Introduction

Before your child starts reading, read this story description. Then look through the book together and talk about the pictures.

This story is called *Fish Makes Faces*. It's about how Fish finds a mirror and then looks at himself making faces.

FISH MAKES FACES

Michelle Knudsen ILLUSTRATED BY Valeria Petrone

C

Fish finds a mirror.

Fish makes a happy face.

Fish makes a sad face.

Fish makes a mad face.

Fish makes a silly face.

Fish makes a scary face.

Fish gets scared!

Fish swims away.